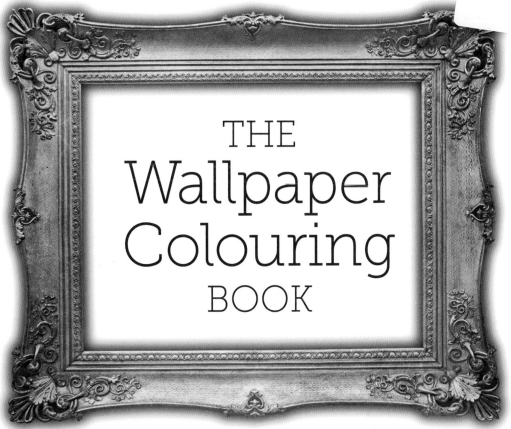

THE
Wallpaper
Colouring
BOOK

"Whatever you have in your rooms think first of the walls for they are that which makes your house and home, and if you do not make some sacrifices in their favour you will find your chambers have a kind of makeshift, lodging-house look about them..."

WILLIAM MORRIS

THE Wallpaper Colouring BOOK

Curated & edited by
Natalia Price-Cabrera

Illustrated by
Gemma Latimer & Jessica Stokes

The Wallpaper Colouring Book

An Hachette UK Company
www.hachette.co.uk

First published in Great Britain in 2015 by
ILEX, a division of Octopus Publishing Group Ltd
Octopus Publishing Group
Carmelite House
50 Victoria Embankment
London, EC4Y 0DZ

www.octopusbooks.co.uk

Copyright © Octopus Publishing Group 2015
Text © Natalia Price-Cabrera
Images © their respective owners
Original book concept devised by Zara Larcombe

Executive Publisher: Roly Allen
Commissioning Editor: Zara Larcombe
Senior Project Editor: Natalia Price-Cabrera
Senior Specialist Editor: Frank Gallaugher
Assistant Editor: Rachel Silverlight
Art Director: Julie Weir
Designer: Kate Haynes
Senior Production Manager: Katherine Hockley

ISBN 978-1-78157-242-9

A CIP catalogue record for this book
is available from the British Library

Printed and bound in China

10 9 8 7 6 5 4 3

CONTENTS

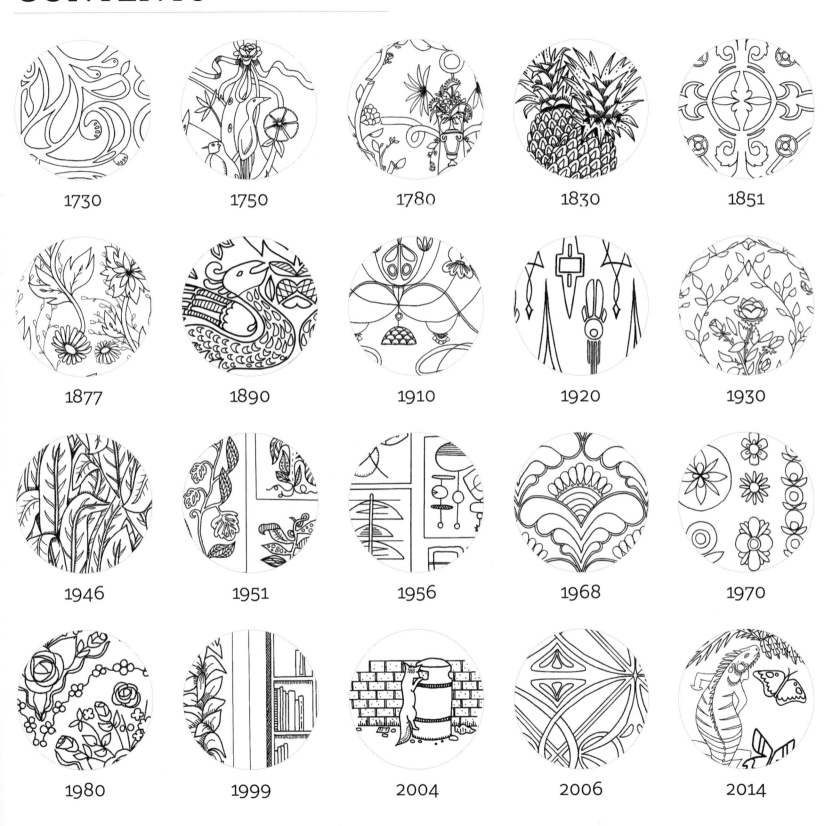

1 Wallpaper by Hugo Goes (ca. 1509)
© Victoria and Albert Museum, London.

2 Wallpaper by A.W.N. Pugin, 1848
© Victoria and Albert Museum, London.

3 *The Day Lily* by Walter Crane, 1897–98
© Victoria and Albert Museum, London.

4 *Acanthus* © www.william-morris.co.uk.

5 *Strawberry Thief*
© www.william-morris.co.uk.

INTRODUCTION

Wallpaper hasn't always been as on trend as it is today. There have been very distinct periods in history when it was considered vulgar and quite the opposite of "fashionable." Thankfully, it is currently experiencing a renaissance and with this book we tap into this zeitgeist and revel in all things wallpaper-related.

You could say that wall "decoration" started way back with the earliest cave paintings some 40,800 years ago—today's equivalent of murals and even graffiti. After this, leather and fabrics were used over walls and openings as insulation to keep the heat in and cold out. Between the 5th and the 15th century, nobility used tapestries in their castles for this purpose. During the late renaissance, fortified castles were not needed and nobility built palaces instead where a great deal of thought was given to interior decor and furniture. Many historians believe wallpaper was introduced as a cheaper substitute to tapestries. It is widely thought that less well-off members of the aristocracy and the emerging merchant class were unable to buy tapestries as a result of either high prices or wars preventing international trade, and thus turned to wallpaper to decorate their homes. Our need to decorate and personalize the space around us would appear to be an inherent characteristic of being human.

The history of wallpaper as we know it today is intrinsically linked to the establishment and development of the paper industry, and wood block-printing techniques. From the 15th century onward, paper making and printmaking were considered extremely important for the dissemination of texts—it was onto the reverse side of condemned literature that nascent wallpaper designs were first printed. The earliest records of wallpaper in the western world can be dated as far back as 1481 with a commission from Louis XI of France. The earliest known wallpaper still in existence dates back to around 1509, but wasn't unearthed until 1911. It was discovered on the ceiling of rooms in Christ's College in Cambridge and was "a formalized pomegranate design inspired by Italian damask," to quote Charlotte Abrahams. [1] It was printed by woodcut on the back of a proclamation issued by Henry VIII and is attributed to Hugo Goes, a York printer.

Early "wallpapers" were individual sheets of waste paper, as mentioned above, with designs printed using wood blocks. Designs were either geometric patterns printed using a single carved wood block or more adventurous patterns incorporating several motifs and printed by several blocks. Designs were printed in black and white, and colored inks were applied with a stencil afterward. These single sheets were known as "Dominos." For single sheets to work as multiple wall coverings and stand the test of time they would need to be joined together. This happened during the 17th century with the emergence of the first continuous rolls made up of 12 joined single sheets pasted together after printing. These roles were approximately 33ft (10m) in length, which remains the standard length of a roll of wallpaper today.

It took almost a century and a great deal of technological wizardry to produce a roll of single sheets pasted together prior to printing. This was a vast milestone in the development of wallpaper and allowed designers to experiment with repeats far greater than the size of an individual sheet. Exciting times indeed. One of the few surviving examples of a large-scale printed pattern of this kind is a rather impressive paper rescued from a builder's dumpster in Epsom during the 1980s.

"WALLPAPER... IS NEITHER NEUTRAL, SAFE NOR BENIGN."

Walls are Talking: Wallpaper Art and Culture Exhibition, Manchester, 2010

With this development came an interesting about turn in the desirability of wallpaper. No longer did wallpaper merely mimic existing surface finishes and textures, such as wood, fabric, and marble; it now came with a very distinct design character of its own and one that was extremely sought after by the wealthy who had previously shunned it. This period saw the British wallpaper industry thrive to such an extent that in 1712 Queen Anne declared it a good of luxury and introduced a tax on paper that was "painted, printed or stained to serve as hangings. To outwit the taxman, wallpapers were colored by hand after being hung on the wall." [2]

Britain didn't hold a monopoly over the wallpaper industry, however, as there was healthy trade of "China Papers" with the Far East, America imported with fervor, and the French certainly took advantage of British taxation with top-end patterns by extremely talented designers aimed at those with money. This was all well and good, but it became very clear by the late 1700s that in order to move forward the industry would have to discover some way of printing a continuous roll using less costly methods with the end

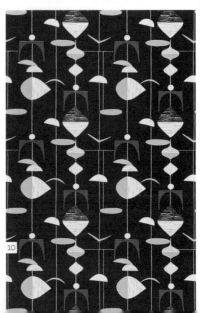

6 *Verdure*, 2012 © www.zoffany.com.

7 *Palace Flock*, Albany Performance, Courtesy www.wallpaperdirect.com.

8 *Tortuga, safran*, 2010 © Manuel Canovas at Colefax and Fowler, www.manuelcanovas.com.

9 *Bengale, paprika*, 2004 © Manuel Canovas at Colefax and Fowler, www.manuelcanovas.com.

10 *Mobiles*, 2011 © www.sanderson-uk.com.

11 *The Dresser*, 2014 by Emma Bridgewater © www.sanderson-uk.com.

12 *Burlesque*, 2009 © www.dupenny.com.

13 *Sugar Skull*, 2015 © www.dupenny.com.

14 *Genuine Fake Bookshelf*, 2005 © www.deborahbowness.com.

15 *Wallpaper Frocks*, 1999 © www.deborahbowness.com. Photograph courtesy of Claire Richardson.

goal of making wallpaper available to the masses. In 1785, Frenchman Christophe-Philippe Oberkampf invented the first wallpaper-printing machine. In 1839 in Britain, Charles Harold Potter invented a four-color printing machine that could turn out 400 rolls of wallpaper a day. "Each color required a separate roller, and synthetic pigments like ultramarine blue and chrome yellow were used on rolls of continuous paper made from wood pulp instead of cotton-on-linen-rag fiber, greatly reducing the manufacturing costs." [3] By 1850 this had increased to eight-color printing, and by 1874 to 20-color printing. Mechanization really was here to stay. With such astounding technological advances, production increased exponentially and prices dropped. Wallpaper was seen as a cheap and very effective way of brightening up cramped and dark rooms in the vast proportion of Victorian homes. "In France, technological advances sparked a fashion for papers featuring trompe-l'oeil swags of opulent fabric, while in Britain, manufacturers used mechanization to produce papers strewn with hyper-real flowers. The average Victorian homeowner loved them, covering living-room walls with cabbage roses so realistic they appeared three-dimensional," [4] details Charlotte Abrahams.

As prolific and intricate as Victorian wallpaper was, the 1920s remain wallpaper's Golden Age. The early 1900s saw the invention of the wallpaper-pasting machine, and in 1920 the first mechanized silk-screen printing machine was developed. An extremely exciting aspect of this decade was that designers not only looked to the past for design inspiration, they also looked to what was going on around them and incorporated cubist and futurist elements in their designs, making them fresh and innovative.

Since the 1930s, the 20th century has had a turbulent relationship with wallpaper. Designers and artists making their mark during this century include Dorothy Draper, Mary Quant, Charles Rennie MacKintosh, Lucienne Day, Peter Hall, Laura Ashley, Sir Terence Conran, Andy Warhol, Celia Birtwell, Vivienne Westwood, and Barbara Hulanicki, to name but a few. The extended captions in the following pages will expand on this in more detail. In the late 1990s, there was a handful of designers hungry to apply new digital technology to the design and manufacture of wallpaper—designers such as Timorous Beasties, Deborah Bowness, Tracy Kendall, and Sharon Elphick.

Today, we refer to wall coverings instead of wallpapers, and these "coverings" are made of all manner of materials and for every budget.

There has been some wonderful high-tech stuff going on over the last few years too, with wallpaper that blocks some mobile phone and WiFi signals in the interest of privacy. "Not only can the new paper stop your neighbors from stealing your bandwidth, but more seriously, it protects your bank details and other sensitive particulars from would-be thieves."[5] Think Big Factory, a Spanish company, has also developed a wallpaper that using motion sensors, projectors, and webcams, serves as a computer interface.

"MY WALLPAPER AND I ARE
FIGHTING A DUEL TO THE
DEATH. ONE OR THE OTHER
OF US HAS TO GO."
The last words spoken by Oscar Wilde

Very 21st century. And in 2012, scientists announced that they had developed a wallpaper strong enough and flexible enough to help stop a masonry wall from falling in the event of an earthquake. Truly remarkable.

Now that you are acquainted with the historical facts, let's get on with the creative bit. This book is a celebration of wallpaper, in which 20 eras have been selected from its rich and colorful history. We have extracted the essence of original wallpaper designs from each era and created completely new and fresh designs that pay homage to past times. These wallpaper backdrops are there for you to color in any which way you like. For the purists among you, there are also color palettes for each era at the back of the book if you want to stay true to what was in vogue at any one time. In addition, a beautiful collage depicting the living space of each era accompanies each wallpaper design, adding a three-dimensional context to the room sets and a witty narrative. Here's to channeling your inner child. Happy coloring!

16 *Prism*, 2013 © www.prestigious.co.uk.

17 *Lustre Tile*, 2012 © www.zoffany.com.

18 *Grand Blotch Damask*, 2013
© www.timorousbeasties.com.

19 *Bloody Hell*, 2007
© www.timorousbeasties.com.

20 *Glasgow Toile*, 2004
© www.timorousbeasties.com.

[1] *The Ultimate Guide: Wallpaper*, 2009 Quadrille Publishing Ltd.
[2] Historic Wallpaper: If walls could talk/http://chezchazz.hubpages.com.
[3] Historic Wallpaper: If walls could talk/http://chezchazz.hubpages.com.
[4] *The Ultimate Guide: Wallpaper*, 2009 Quadrille Publishing Ltd.
[5] www.ft.com.

1730

The 1730s heralded the rise of flock papers. Flock is powdered wool, which was a byproduct of the wool industry. Sticky size was applied in patterns to sheets of paper, and it was then covered with woolen fibers that had been shredded and dyed, which stuck to the size to produce a raised surface pattern. Originally invented to imitate the look and feel of damask, cut-velvet, and other textile wall hangings, these flock papers proved to be extremely durable, and as a result, the fact that production was a labor-intensive process and they were expensive seemed to matter not. Flock papers were also extremely successful at repelling moths due to the turpentine in the adhesive. The design of flock wallpaper has adapted over the centuries to reflect trends in fashion and textile design. Sadly, its popularity went into decline during Queen Victoria's reign, although many beautiful flocks are still being produced for restoration projects and residential use today. In the mid-to-late 1700s, many flocks were designed with grand, formal spaces in mind, and were produced in large pattern repeats that could be up to 7ft (2.1m) in length. A backlash to the severity of the Baroque style preceding it, rococo designs were very popular at this time and included delicate, feminine motifs such as flowers, vases, scroll work, asymmetrical and Oriental designs, and natural patterns.

1750

Chinoiserie was very fashionable in 1750. Derived from "Chinois," the French for Chinese, the style was a fusion of design from China, Japan, and other Asian countries. Imported goods from these countries—seen as strange, wonderful, far-off places—were very sought after in the 18th century. As a result, many designers and craftsmen looked to the porcelain, lacquer ware, and silks as a source of inspiration, and created their own fanciful versions of Chinese figures, pagodas, fabulous birds, exotic flowers, dragons, and foliage, and injected an element of fantasy. The Chinese Room in Claydon House is probably the most elaborate surviving Chinoiserie interior in Britain. Chinoiserie was closely related to the rococo style, and both are styles often seen used in conjunction with one another in interior design.

Jean Pillement (1728–1808), a French artist and some-time royal painter to Marie Antoinette who settled in London in 1750, was a hugely influential designer of Chinoiserie decoration. He published two collections of prints, in 1755 and 1767, which were subsequently copied and adapted for wallpaper designs. Interestingly, Pillement never actually traveled to Asia. His interpretations of Asian design were gleaned from travel books written by other Europeans, hence his highly original designs.

1780

The late 18th century is considered to be the Golden Age of French wallpaper. Jean-Baptiste Réveillon (1725–1811) was a French wallpaper manufacturer who hired the best designers working in silk and tapestry to produce some of the most luxurious wallpapers ever created at this time. In 1775, he opened a paper mill to improve the quality and quantity of his papers. His *papier bleu d'Angleterre* became very popular after Queen Marie Antoinette decorated her apartments with them. In 1783 Réveillon was given permission to go by the moniker of *Manufacture Royale*. The same year, Réveillon's sky-blue wallpaper with fleurs-de-lys was emblazoned on the first hot-air balloons by the Montgolfier brothers.

Probably the most interesting aspect of late 18th-century wallpaper design is the emergence of flowers as a decorative motif. Of course, flowers have been used in decoration before this, but by 1780 they took on a prominence not seen previously. Instead of being just a secondary or background detail, flowers became elevated as the subject of many wallpaper designs. Designs were naturalistic in style and based heavily on the realistic and abundant approach of the Flemish flower painters of this period.

Designers and manufacturers at this time included Jean-Baptiste Fay (active c. 1885) and Joseph Laurent Malaine (1745–1809).

1830

Throughout North America in the 1800s, architects, designers, and craftsmen alike rapidly adopted the pineapple as a design motif. European colonists had begun importing this exotic fruit to the US from the Caribbean in the 1700s. Due to its rareness, it was expensive to buy and it quickly became a symbol of wealth. The trade routes between the US and the Caribbean were notoriously dangerous, so it was customary for sea captains to place a pineapple outside their homes as a sign of their safe return. Over time, the pineapple became a dominant design motif, symbolizing warmth and hospitality, and was incorporated into all manner of home furnishings—from furniture, to wallpapers, to table linen.

Also fashionable at this time was trompe-l'oeil wallpaper made to look like drapery, and padded, buttoned upholstery. Thrown into the mix was a mash-up of motifs adopted from previous historical periods never witnessed before.

Sadly, 1830 saw the wallpaper manufacturer Joseph Dufour et Cie shut its doors for the last time (1797–1830). Arthur et Robert, a Paris-based wallpaper manufacturer exporting their products throughout Europe and North America, continued to block print fabulous trompe-l'oeil wallpapers, as did Zuber et Cie, a company still in existence today.

1851

By 1851, Queen Victoria had been on the throne for 14 years and Victorian ideals were fairly well ingrained. Indeed, it was at the Great Exhibition in London that Victorian inventions and morals were first put on show for the entire world to see. Decorative illusion and deception were frowned upon, so wallpapers imitating wood grain, fabric, or marble were considered "dishonest material." This new mindset paved the way for the Design Reform.

A key player at this time was Welsh architect and designer Owen Jones (1809–1874). His theories on color and flat patterning are still relevant today. Jones drew on his travels to Europe, in particular the Alhambra in Spain, which heavily influenced his love of Islamic decoration. *The Grammar of Ornament*—a collection of his drawings, flat patterning, geometry, abstraction in ornamentation, and color theories—was published in 1856 and is still in print today.

Another leading figure at this time was A.W.N. Pugin (1812–52), who embraced all things Gothic, believing this to be the true British style. He deplored the use of trompe-l'oeil, instead championing flat patterns composed of simple forms such as fleurs-de-lis, heraldic motifs, and quatrefoils, all printed in rich colors. Pugin's wallpaper designs were better suited to more formal spaces, while Jones' wallpaper designs were more popular for domestic interiors.

1877

During the latter part of the 19th century, the English wallpaper producer Jeffrey & Co championed the work of various artists and designers involved in the Arts and Crafts movement. Walter Crane (1845–1915) was one such artist. A prolific designer and illustrator, his designs were translated into textiles, ceramics, and wallpapers, and were very popular with the general public. Crane was influenced by Japanese art and this was evident in his wallpaper designs. His designs are characterized by flat colors and crisp outlines.

By the late 1870s, it had become very popular and financially lucrative for commercial artists to freelance their talents and designs out to wallpaper companies. A busy designer could earn up to £400 per year, which was a substantial amount of money in those days. As a result of this, wallpaper companies could offer a far greater number of wallpapers and styles than ever before, catering for an increasingly discerning audience. In 1880, Silver Studio was founded by Arthur Silver. It became one of the leading textile design studios in England until the mid-20th century, producing designs for Liberty, Warner and Sons Ltd., and Sanderson.

Designers at this time included William Burges (1827–1881), Christopher Dresser (1834–1904), Lewis F. Day (1845–1910), and B. J. Talbert (1838–1881).

1890

The Arts and Crafts movement was made up of English designers and writers who wanted a return to well-made, handcrafted goods instead of mass-produced, poor-quality, machine-made items. Inspired by socialist principles and led by William Morris (1834–1896), the members of the movement used the medieval system of trades and guilds to set up their own companies to sell their goods. Unfortunately, it had the reverse effect and, apart from the wealthy middle classes, hardly anyone could afford their designs. Not everyone approved of the aesthetics—Oscar Wilde apparently wrote to a friend saying, "I don't at all agree with you about the decorative value of Morris's wallpapers. They seem to me often deficient in real beauty of color... I have seen far more rooms spoiled by wallpapers than by anything else."

Visually, the style had much in common with its contemporary, Art Nouveau, which emerged from Paris at the same time. William Morris designs are still very fashionable today. Also popular around this time were Lincrusta and Anaglypta papers. Anaglypta was developed by Thomas Palmer in 1887. It is essentially embossed patterned wallpaper used below the dado rail and ideal for painting.

Designers at this time included CFA Voysey (1857–1941) and John Henry Dearle (1859–1898).

1910

From 1890 onward, there was growing resistance to the Arts and Crafts movement and the insular nature of this very English and academic decorative style. Emerging in France at the Paris Exposition Universelle in 1900, Art Nouveau—"new art"—is considered the first original modern style of the 20th century, as it shunned nostalgia and embraced the here and now. Designers stopped looking to the past and instead took inspiration from what was around them in the natural world. Art Nouveau is a very distinctive style recognized by its organic shapes and abstraction, and is now valued as an important stepping stone between the historic revival styles of the late 19th century and the Modernist styles of the 20th century.

By 1910, Art Nouveau interior design was thought of as the height of fashion and design excellence, with wallpaper playing a major role. Seen as a "total" art style, Art Nouveau was applied to the decorative arts as a whole. Arthur Lasenby Liberty, founder of Liberty in London, helped nurture Art Nouveau to such an extent that in Italy, Art Nouveau was known as "Stile Liberty."

Designers at this time included Hector Guimard (1867–1942), Charles Rennie Mackintosh (1868–1928), Josef Hoffmann (1870–1956), and Hans Christiansen (1866–1945).

1920

Art Deco emerged as a style during the interwar years spanning the heyday of the "roaring" 1920s and the decline of the Depression-ridden 1930s. The label Art Deco is thought to have been derived from the Exposition Internationale des Art Décoratifs et Industriels Modernes held in Paris in 1925. As a style, Art Deco was all about luxury, glamour, and mass production. One major trait differentiating it from its predecessor, Art Nouveau, is that it embraced technology. Design motifs of this decade were bold—lightning bolts, sun rays, stepped forms, and stylized, two-dimensional flowers. The influence of Futurism, Cubism, Constructivism, African art, and even Diaghilev's *Ballets Russes* was also very evident in design at this time.

In 1919, designer Émile-Jacques Ruhlmann (1879–1933) founded Ruhlmann et Laurent with Pierre Laurent. The company specialized in interior design, focusing on wallpaper, lighting, and furniture, and produced only the highest-quality goods. Ruhlmann's valuable contribution to the history of design was recognized in 2004, when he was the subject of a major retrospective exhibition at the Metropolitan Museum of Art in New York in 2004, and in 2009 *The New York Times* referred to him as "Art Deco's greatest artist."

Designers at this time included Wenzel Hablik (1881–1934), Maurice Dufrène (1876–1955), and Josef Margold (1888–1962).

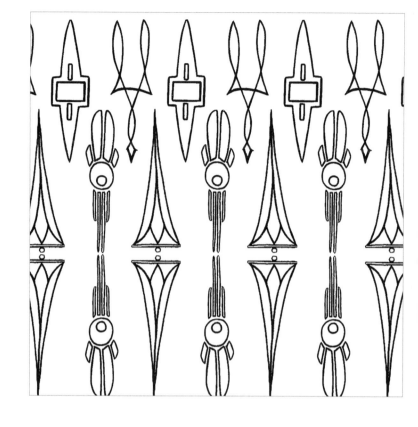

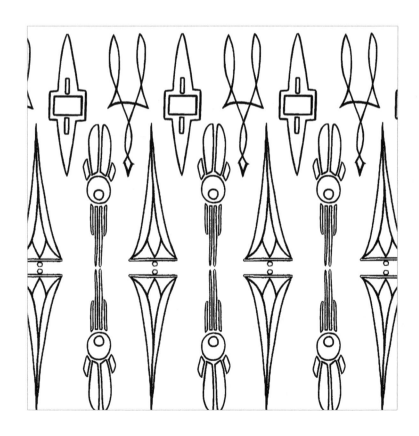

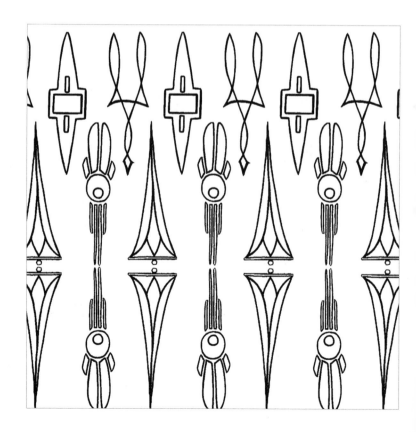

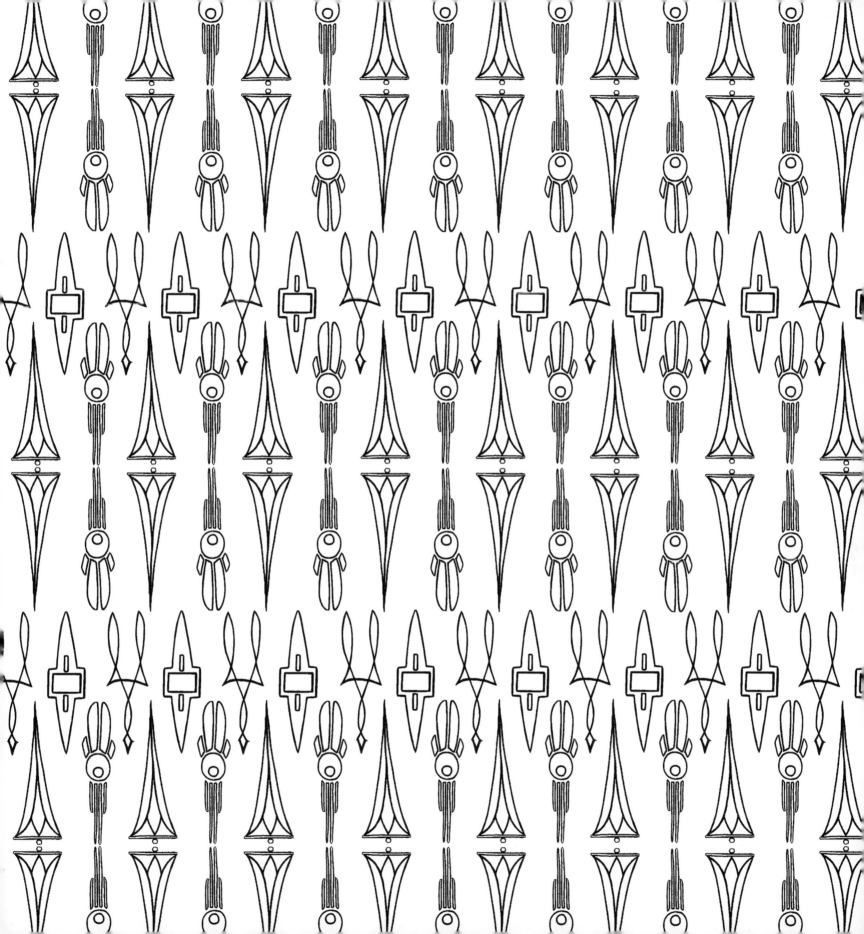

1930

During the 1930s, there were several strands of design influences at play. To many, the early 1930s was all about celebrating the mechanized, modern world. However, this was also the time of the Great Depression and the run-up to the Second World War, and there were many designers who turned their back on all this "Modernism" and instead looked to the past for inspiration. This faction took established wallpaper motifs, such as flowers or other historical styles, and reinterpreted them to create contemporary wallpaper designs. One designer "flying in the face of Modernist abstraction," according to Lesley Jackson, was English designer Edward Bawden (1903–1989). His design, called *Conservatory*, "juxtaposed vases of flowers with doll-like Victorian figures." Bawden was a great fan of early 19th-century motifs and often referenced these in his designs.

By the mid-1930s, textured wallpapers were developed. They sported three-dimensional, machine-embossed muted patterns, and were known as "porridge." With the outbreak of war in 1939, developments in wallpaper design and manufacturing ground to a halt due to shortages and would not resurface until the mid-1940s.

Designers at this time included Raymond McGrath (1903–1977), Paul Schultze-Naumburg (1869–1949), Ilonka Karasz (1896–1981), and Marion Dorn (1896–1964).

1946

Creativity in the early 1940s was overshadowed by the Second World War and a shortage of materials. By 1946, with the war over, production started to pick up. Design-wise, there was a creative boom as people embraced life again. Rationing was a distant memory and there was money to be spent on home interiors. Designs were exotic and flamboyant, incorporating florals, foliage, and lots of ruffles.

Designer and decorator Don Loper created the now-legendary *Martinique Banana Leaf* wallpaper in 1942 for the Beverly Hills Hotel, which is still iconic to this day and can be seen in Martin Scorsese's film, *The Aviator* (2004). Possibly my favorite wallpaper of this decade, though, is American designer Dorothy Draper's *Brazilliance*, used to great effect at the Greenbrier Hotel in West Virginia. The entire design scheme at the Greenbrier is testament to the abundance of creativity at this period in history. In 2007, its design was refreshed by Dorothy Draper's protégé Carleton Varney. This style of wallpaper is still very much in fashion today and the Greenbrier Hotel itself was used as the backdrop to Bergdorf Goodman's Fall 2012 advertising campaign.

Manufacturers at this time included Graham & Brown, which was founded in 1946 by close friends Harold Graham and Henry Brown.

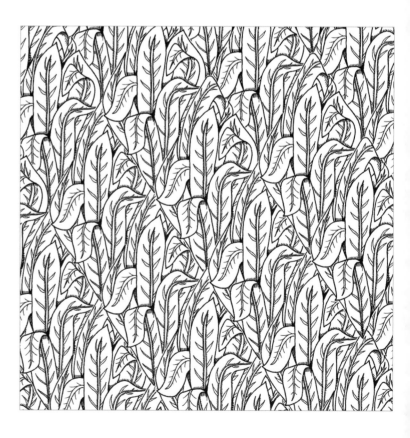

1951

The design here is typical of the style of Mary White, a leading fabric and wallpaper designer in the 1950s. White was very influenced by the designs of William Morris, studying books of flowers and the countryside where she grew up. This design is close to her famous *Cottage Garden*, which sold in London's fashionable Heal's store, and was fortunate to come on the market at a time when people were looking to freshen up their homes with the new post-war aesthetic. Practical innovations continued at this time too. Vinyl wallpapers were launched in the late 1940s, and in the 1950s pre-pasted papers were introduced.

The summer of 1951 saw the Festival of Britain held across the United Kingdom. Organized by the government, the exhibition was a post-war celebration of British arts, architecture, industrial design, technology, and science. John Line's *Limited Editions* collection was launched at the Festival. The collection featured screen-printed and block-printed wallpaper designs by designers such as William Odell, Sylvia Priestley (1894–1984), Lucienne Day (1917–2010), and Henry Skeen.

Wallpaper designers at this time included Jacqueline Groag (1903–1985) and Diana Armfield (1920–).

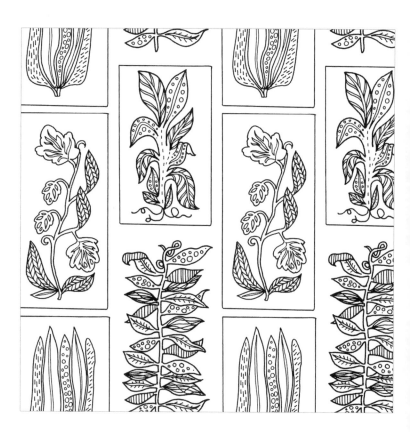

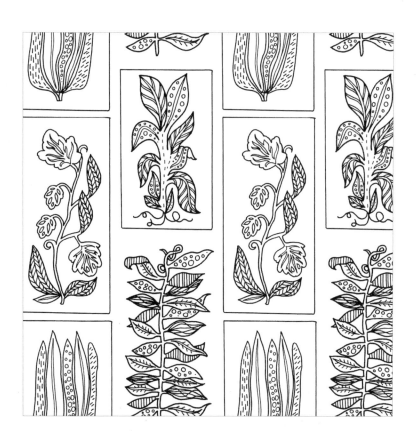

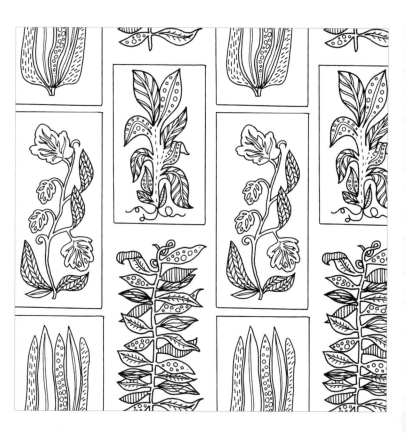

1956

By the mid-1950s, wallpaper designs reflected a widespread fascination with technology, science, modern art, and all things futuristic. According to Joanne Kosuda Warner, "the papers considered most modern...were those covered with doodles, squiggles, loops, sound waves, prisms, vertical graphs, Miró-like forms, amoeba, and even flying saucers." These contemporary wallpapers became increasingly popular thanks to the growing production and consumption of women's magazines. A major focus of these magazines was on interior design, and a great deal of space was given over to promoting these modern designs.

Hailing from America, the idea of a "feature wall" was born. Many contemporary wallpaper designs were so bold and colorful that to have them on every wall would have been too much for the average homeowner. More subdued papers were used on other walls in a room to balance the overall effect. Open-plan living was ever more fashionable—again an import from America—and these vibrant, modern papers helped zone different living spaces within a home.

Similar to the "Design Reform" of the mid-19th century, the 1950s had its own "Good Design" movement, encouraging companies to elevate the importance of the designer responsible for a wallpaper design—often anonymous in the case of mass-produced papers.

1968

The wallpaper here is typical of the large-scale repeats by the designer Peter Hall, whose striking papers and clashing colors graced the walls of many homes in the late 1960s and 1970s. Yet again, Hall was strongly influenced by the styles of William Morris, taking his curvaceous forms to stylized heights. Typical colors were dark greens, yellows, pinks, and oranges, even purple and cobalt blue, creating rooms that these days are considered lurid and overbearing. As Mary Quant eloquently said, "I love vulgarity. Good taste is death, vulgarity is life."

The 1960s also saw the introduction of new technologies that would revolutionize the wallpaper industry. Vinyl wallpaper, although more expensive than conventional wallpapers, had the biggest impact and was favored in offices, hotels, and hospitals. The general homeowner also found them attractive for use in kitchens and bathrooms due to their washable nature. According to Joanne Kosuda Warner, "by 1967, mass-produced wallpaper was pre-pasted, pre-trimmed, and easily stripped," which was clearly targeted at the DIY market and became very popular indeed.

Designers at this time included Barbara Brown (1939–) and Shirley Craven (1934–), and Osborne & Little's first collection was launched in London in 1968.

1970

The 1970s has sometimes been referred to as the decade that time forgot, but I beg to differ. The 1970s represented a fusion of flower power, psychedelic patterns, and an Art Nouveau and Art Deco revivalism, coupled with a large dollop of Op Art and Pop Art influence. Wallpaper designs were decadent, bold, and completely over the top. The color palette was equally striking, featuring garish pinks, mauves, and reds. This era was all about extremes in terms of design, particularly in interior decor.

Metallic surfaces were also very fashionable, so paper-backed foil, Mylar, vinyl-coated foil, and metallic pigments became increasingly popular in wall coverings. However, they were pricey so were not usually found in the home; instead they adorned hotels, restaurants, and retail spaces.

The design shown here is a floral one, typical of this period. Stylized, almost geometric flowers on a fairly tight repeat often characterized these large-scale patterns.

Designers at this time included Osborne & Little (known for its trademark hand screen-printed designs), Tricia Guild (founded Designers Guild in 1970 with Robin Guild and has collaborated with artists such as Kaffe Fassett, Lillian Delavoryas, and Janice Tchalenko), and David Hicks (1929–1998).

1980

Although often associated with the mid-to-late 1970s, Laura Ashley's (1925–1985) popularity continued well into the 1980s, with 70 stores worldwide. Her nostalgic designs were inspired by 19th-century pattern books, conjuring up a romanticized, bucolic way of life in which flower and leaf motifs predominated. According to Iain Gale and Susan Irvine, in their book *Laura Ashley Style*, "she brought poetry and fantasy back into ordinary domestic life, liberating design from chrome, plastics, and man-made fibers." Indeed, Laura Ashley's rise to fame had a great deal to do with the fact that she flew in the face of all things artificial and futuristic. A fan of natural fabrics, she provided the complete interior solution in terms of supplying wallpapers, bed linen, curtains, cushions, upholstery fabrics, and table linen.

Helping to cement the whole country-house style was a renewed love for the National Trust, which in turn brought about a new admiration for all things chintz. And in 1986, Britain's wallpaper history society was established.

Designers at this time included Sue Timney (who founded Timney Fowler in 1980 with Grahame Fowler), and Susan Collier and Sarah Campbell of Collier Campbell (who produced an annual collection of wallpapers for Habitat from 1980 until 1992).

1999

The 1990s was an exciting decade of brave new design as a new generation of artists and designers rediscovered the beauty of wallpaper, pushing the boundaries further than ever before. One such artist-designer was Deborah Bowness, who graduated from the Royal College of Art in 1999 with an MA in constructed textiles. It was during her time at the RCA that Deborah was first inspired to challenge preconceived ideas of wallpaper. Harnessing advances in digital technology and playing around with photorealism, Deborah produced a body of work called *Hooks & Frocks*, allowing her to create "functional art." She combined photographs of hanging dresses—put together in a montage and printed digitally—with real hooks, and then added silk-screened color and hand-painted details to create exquisite panels of contemporary trompe-l'oeil. According to Deborah, it was a "deliberate shun of the repeat pattern. [She] never intended her work to dominate a room. Rather, it was to sit quietly, playfully interacting with the objects and furniture around it."

Designers at this time included Sharon Elphick (1968–), Tracy Kendall, Jocelyn Warner (formed in 1999), David Oliver (whose wallpaper design *Liberation* was launched in 1998), and Timorous Beasties (founded in 1990).

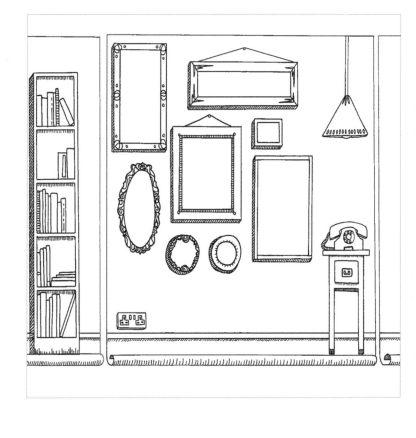

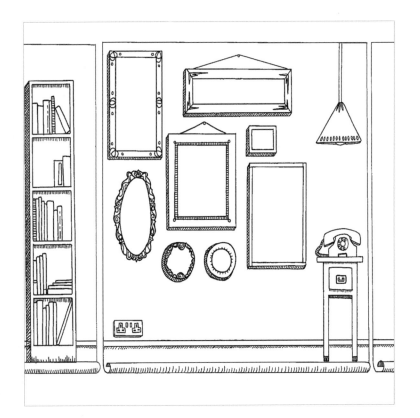

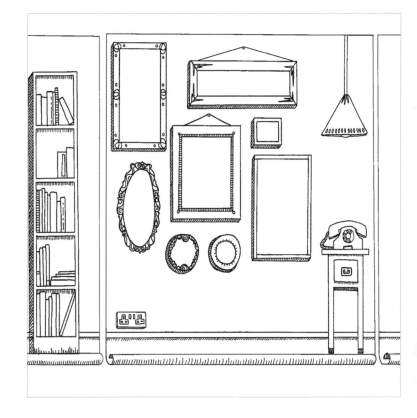

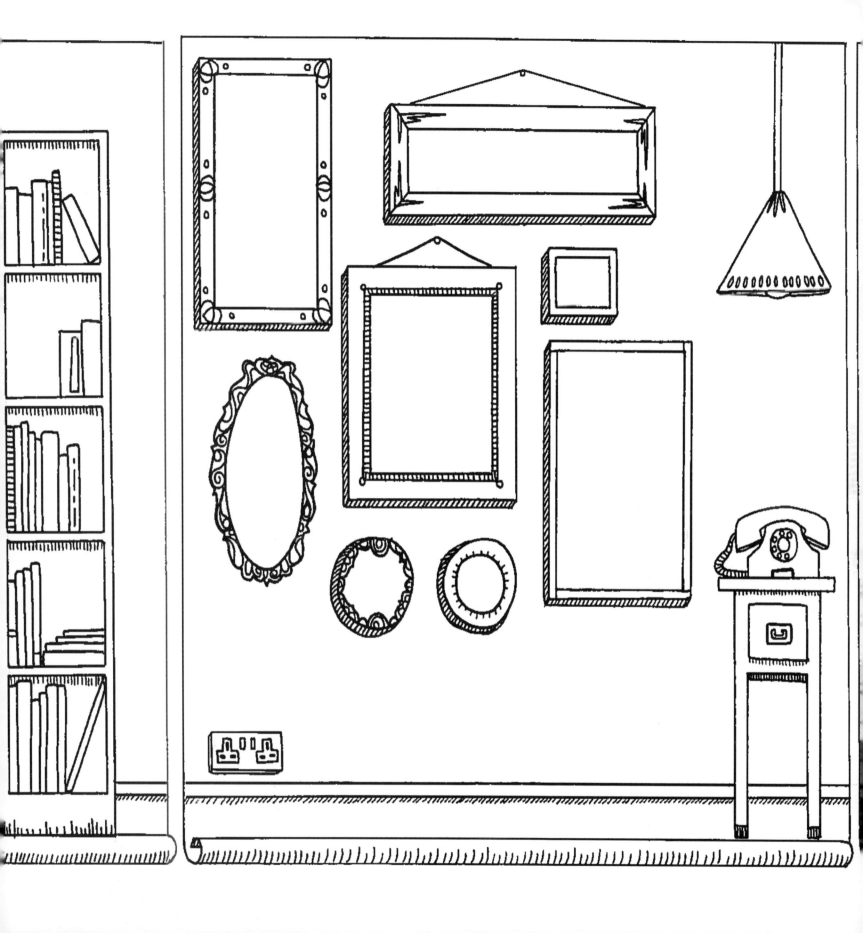

2004

The design shown here is based on Timorous Beasties' critically acclaimed *Glasgow Toile*, which was unveiled in 2004. Founded in 1990 by Glasgow-based creative duo Paul Simmons and Alistair McAuley, Timorous Beasties (the name is taken from a Robert Burns' poem), has been raising the design bar ever since.

Glasgow Toile proved a revelation—a contemporary take on the traditional and revered French toile de Jouy. However, this time it was gritty, urban Glasgow landmarks that featured in the design, depicting a "darker side of urban social realism," according to Simon Clarke in *Print: Fashion, Interiors, Art*. Most of Timorous Beasties' designs are produced as both textiles and wallpapers, and it also has a range of lampshades sporting them. Collections are printed to order using different printing methods, but always designing for the process in mind. The pair's design philosophy sees plants, animals, and society as visually inextricable. They are devoted to how this affects pattern design in our daily experience of furnished spaces, regardless of the scale of the space.

Designers at this time included Manuel Canovas, Abigail Lane (1967–), Dorkenwald-Spitzer, and Maya Romanoff (1941–2014)—an award-winning innovator famous for his flexible, glass-beaded surface material called "Bedazzled," and metallic-leafed papers.

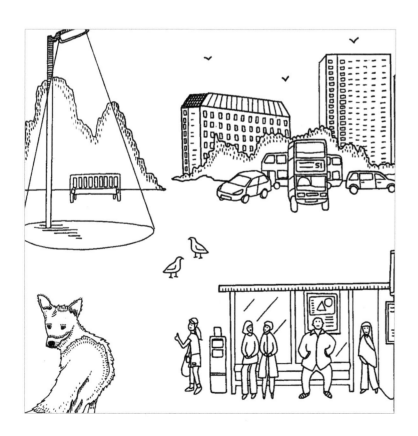

2006

The design shown here is inspired by Barbara Hulaniki's wallpaper designs. Hulaniki (1936–) is a design-world icon, famous for her store and brand Biba, launched in 1964. The store became the go-to place for the rich and famous, and was lavishly decorated in an Art Nouveau and Art Deco style. Her wallpaper designs are based on her illustrative work, which in turn is heavily influenced by her love of Celtic motifs and all things Art Nouveau. In 2006 Hulaniki collaborated with Habitat to produce a very popular collection of wallpapers. She has also designed wallpapers for Graham & Brown since 2003. Luxurious materials, such as metallics and sumptuous flocks, characterize Hulaniki's wallpaper designs. There is also an element of the Gothic in designs such as *Skulls Black*, *Diablo Raven*, and *Maleficent Midnight*.

Celia Birtwell (1941–)—also famous in the 1960s due to her fashionable textile designs for her then-husband, fashion designer Ossie Clarke—launched her first wallpaper collection in 2006. The collection was based on two designs called *Jacobean* and *Beasties*, and was heavily influenced by 17th-century antique textiles. This collection proved extremely popular.

Designers at this time included Thomas Demand (2006 wallpaper design *Efeu*) and Tres Tintas Barcelona.

2014

This design pays homage to the beautiful and exotic wallpaper designs of House of Hackney and Witch & Watchman. House of Hackney—a company founded in London in 2010 by husband-and-wife team Javvy M Royle and Frieda Gormley—has a mission "to take the beige out of interiors." Its British-made collections of textiles and wallpapers are steeped in tradition, yet bold and subversive, for a truly modern statement. Witch & Watchman was founded in London in 2014 by Helen Z B Wilson, an artist and designer. Helen's striking designs were featured in the "Best new-season fabrics and wallpapers" in *Elle Decoration*'s October 2014 issue. Each design is originally painted by hand in oil on canvas and then digitally printed onto wallpaper and fabric. Helen's passion for painting birds, animals, and flowers, coupled with a long-standing love of the "maximalist" wallpapers and fabrics found in stately homes, fuels her design. Looking to create designs that resemble a modern take on chinoiserie, Witch & Watchman is about bold prints that make a statement.

Designers of note include Flavor Paper (named "Best of New York 2012, Wallpaper" by *New York* magazine), Emily Dupen (Dupenny), Howard Wakefield and Sarah Parris (Parris Wakefield Additions), and Black Crow Studio.

COLOR SWATCHES

For the purists among you. If you would like to stay true to what was on trend here is a selection of color references for each of the eras featured in this book. You can use each color palette as a starting point for your color schemes.

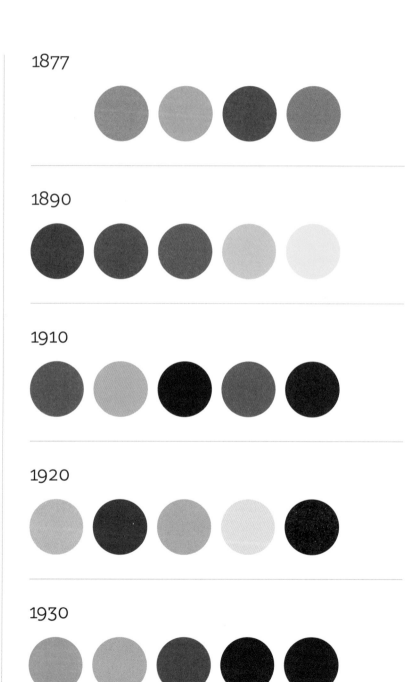

1730

1750

1780

1830

1851

1877

1890

1910

1920

1930

1946

1951

1956

1968

1970

1980

1999

2004

2006

2014

1730

1750

1851

1877

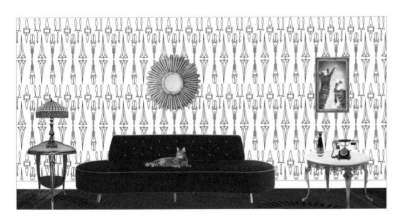

1920

1930

1780

1830

1890

1910

1946

1951

1956

1968

1980

1999

2006

2014

1970

2004

RESOURCES

BOOKS

Pattern Design: A Period Design Sourcebook
Sian Evans, National Trust Books, 2008

20th Century Pattern Design: Textile & Wallpaper Pioneers
(New Edition), Lesley Jackson, Princeton Architectural Press, 2011

Wallpaper: Dreams of Colour for the Home
Alejandro Asensio, Parragon, 2007

The Papered Wall: The History, Patterns & Techniques of Wallpaper
(Second Edition), Lesley Hoskins, Thames & Hudson Ltd., 2005

Wallpaper: The Ultimate Guide
Charlotte Abrahams, Quadrille Publishing Ltd., 2009

Print: Fashion, Interiors, Art,
Simon Clarke, Laurence King Publishing Ltd., 2014

WEBSITES

www.blackcrowstudios.com
www.brewers.co.uk
www.cole-and-son.com
www.colefax.com
www.cooperhewitt.org
www.deborahbowness.com
www.designhistorysociety.org
www.dupenny.com
www.english-heritage.org.uk
www.follyandglee.bigcartel.com
www.geffrye-museum.org.uk
www.gemmalatimer.com
www.grahambrown.com
www.harlequin.uk.com
www.houseofhackney.com
www.manuelcanovas.com
www.millersantiquesguide.com
www.moda.mdx.ac.uk
www.museepapierpeint.org

www.nationaltrust.org.uk
www.osborneandlittle.com
www.parriswakefieldadditions.com
www.prestigious.co.uk
www.sanderson-uk.com
www.sharonelphick.com
www.surfaceprint.com
www.timorousbeasties.com
www.tracykendall.com
www.vam.ac.uk
www.wallpaperdirect.com
www.wallpaperhistorysociety.org.uk
whatjess.drew.blogspot.co.uk
www.william-morris.co.uk
www.witchandwatchman.com
www.zoffany.com
www.zuber.fr

ACKNOWLEDGMENTS

This book has been a collaborative tour de force and as such I have a great many people to thank.

A huge thank you to the extremely talented Zara Larcombe, Commissioning Editor at Ilex/OPG, for coming up with the book's concept in the first place and tirelessly developing it until it was just right. I must also say thank you to the rest of the Ilex/OPG team— Julie Weir, Frank Gallaugher, Rachel Silverlight, Roly Allen, and Adam Juniper—it is a genuine pleasure to work with you, and you make the trek up to London worthwhile!

Another big thank you to Jessica Stokes and Gemma Latimer for their combined creative brilliance. Jessica designed the 20 wallpaper designs featured in this book, while Gemma created the collaged room sets for each era. You have both been a joy to work with and it is always a delight to collaborate with such talented people! A particularly enormous thank you to the very lovely Kate Haynes of Grafikista, who is a dream to work with. Kate has spent more hours than I can count designing this book and pulling a great many disparate elements together to form a cohesive whole. It has been a very labor-intensive process, at the end of which she sprinkled some of her famous design magic to deliver what I believe to be a truly beautiful colouring book. Thank you Kate!

As a result of the generosity and kindness of a number of people, we have been able to feature some truly stunning examples of wallpaper design in this book. So a very big thank you to: Alice Moschetti, Licensing Executive at V&A Images; Hannah Mitchell, Studio Assistant at Timorous Beasties; Deborah Bowness; Miriam Bennett, E-Commerce Administrator at Brewers; Emily Dupen, Owner and Designer at Dupenny; Trudi Ballard, Head of Public Relations and Advertising and Gavin Horton, Press and Marketing Coordinator at Colefax and Fowler; Katie Dick, Marketing Assistant at Prestigious Textiles Ltd.; and Scarlett Ward, PR Assistant at Sanderson, Morris & Co. & Zoffany. Thank you also to Polly Kettley of Folly & Glee for generously donating photographs of some of her fabulous lampshades for use in the book, and to Chris Gatcum for allowing us to feature his photographs as well.

I would also like to thank all my friends and family for their constant belief in me. And there aren't enough thank yous in the world for Chris, Tati, and Georgia-Mae. Let's just say I love you always and forever, and life would be very dull without you all.

Finally in keeping with the narrative of this book, the three feline loves of my life—Pepper, Lemmy, and Halle—deserve a mention as they have been a welcome distraction while working on this project. They have become very accomplished at paper surfing across my desk and it is hilarious to witness.   *Natalia Price-Cabrera*

PICTURE CREDITS:

Front cover: Womb Chair © Knoll. Courtesy of Judith Miller; Gold vintage frame © Luisa Fumi/www.shutterstock.com; Pug dog © Pavel Hlystov/www.shutterstock.com. All images reproduced in this book © www.shutterstock.com unless otherwise indicated.

Prelims: Lampshade courtesy of Folly & Glee Lampshades. Photograph © Polly Kettley. **Introduction:** (1) Wallpaper by Hugo Goes (ca. 1509) © Victoria and Albert Museum, London; (2) Wallpaper by A.W.N. Pugin (1812–52), manufactured by Samuel Scott. Woodblock print. London, England, 1848. © Victoria and Albert Museum, London; (3)The Day Lily by Walter Crane, 1897–98 © Victoria and Albert Museum, London; (4) Acanthus DARW212550 © www.william-morris.co.uk. The wallpaper was launched in the 2013 Archive II collection; (5) Strawberry Thief DARW212550 © www.william-morris.co.uk. The wallpaper was launched in the 2013 Archive II collection; (6) Verdure 310431, from the 2012 Arden collection © www.zoffany.com; (7) Albany Performance, Palace Flock £85.50 available from wallpaperdirect.com. Courtesy of www.wallpaperdirect.com; (8) Tortuga, safran, from the Bellegarde collection, 2010 © Manuel Canovas at Colefax and Fowler, www.manuelcanovas.com; (9) Bengale, paprika, from the Cerisy collection, 2004 © Manuel Canovas at Colefax and Fowler, www.manuelcanovas.com; (10) Mobiles 210214, from the 50s collection, 2011 © www.sanderson-uk.com; (11) The Dresser 213650, from the Emma Bridgewater by Sanderson collection, 2014 © www.sanderson-uk.com; (12) Burlesque, 2009 © www.dupenny.com; (13) Sugar Skull, 2015 © www.dupenny.com; (14) Genuine Fake Bookshelf, 2005 © www.deborahbowness.com; (15) Wallpaper Frocks, 1999 © www.deborahbowness.com. Photograph courtesy of Claire Richardson; (16) Urban Wallcoverings collection, 2013 for spring/summer launch, Prism in colorway Onyx, £79.90 per roll © www.prestigious.co.uk; (17) Lustre Tile 310986, from the Quartz collection, 2012 © www.zoffany.com; (18) Grand Blotch Damask, 2013 © www.timorousbeasties.com; (19) Bloody Hell, 2007 © www.timorousbeasties.com; (20) Glasgow Toile, 2004 © www.timorousbeasties.com.

1750: Pet portraits © Gemma Latimer; George II Tea Table © Bonhams. **1780:** Pet portrait © Gemma Latimer; German Occasional Table © Bonhams. **1830:** Pet portrait © Gemma Latimer. **1851:** Pet portrait © Gemma Latimer; Gothic Style Mantle Clock © Bonhams. **1877:** Pet portraits © Gemma Latimer. **1910:** Pet portrait © Gemma Latimer. **1930:** Lampshade courtesy of Folly & Glee Lampshades. Photograph © Polly Kettley. **1946:** Pet portrait © Gemma Latimer; Lampshades courtesy of Folly & Glee Lampshades. Photograph © Polly Kettley. **1951:** Pet portrait © Gemma Latimer; Pendant lampshade courtesy of Folly & Glee Lampshades. Photograph © Polly Kettley. **1956:** Magazines courtesy of Gemma Latimer; Cushions courtesy of Mols & Tati-Lois. Photograph © Chris Gatcum; Swan sofa image provided courtesy of Republic of Fritz Hansen. **1968:** Artwork on magazine cover © Gemma Latimer; Lampshade courtesy of Folly & Glee Lampshades. Photograph © Polly Kettley. **1970:** Lampshade courtesy of Folly & Glee Lampshades. Photograph © Polly Kettley. **1999:** Cushions and lampshade courtesy of Mols & Tati-Lois. Photograph © Chris Gatcum. **2004:** Lampshade courtesy of Folly & Glee Lampshades. Photograph © Polly Kettley. **2006:** Skull cushion courtesy of Mols & Tati-Lois. Photograph © Chris Gatcum. **2014:** Cushions and lampshade courtesy of Mols & Tati-Lois. Photograph © Chris Gatcum; Womb Chair © Knoll. Courtesy of Judith Miller.

FOR KEVIN
With your beautifully warm nature, playful temperament & big ginger belly. Love always x G.L.